JUST A DOG

P9-CFS-643

MICHAEL GERARD BAUER

SCHOLASTIC INC.

This book was originally published in hardcover by Scholastic Press in 2012.

ISBN 978-0-545-37453-8

12 11 10 9 8 7 6 5 4 3 2 1   14 15 16 17 18 19/0

Printed in the U.S.A. 40
This edition first printing, September 2014

The text was set in Alisal.
The display type is Linotype Centenniel.
Book design by Whitney Lyle
Title page art © 2012 by Jennifer Taylor

**For Toby, Penny, Kim,
and Chloe — good dogs all**

CONTENTS

1

THE STORIES OF MISTER MOSELY

The day my dad said Mister Mosely was "just a dog," my mum punched him.

Not a punch like the one Dad gave Uncle Gavin that time when Uncle Gavin's tooth came out and there was all the blood and everything. But not a girl punch or a fooling-around punch either. Mum really meant it. You could tell by the way she scrunched her face right up and made her eyes go small.

"Don't you *say* that! Don't you *dare* say *that!*"

That's what my mum said while she was punching my dad. She hit him about three times right on the chest and Dad didn't try to stop her or anything. He just stood there and let her, like it was exactly what she should be doing. I guess what my dad did sounds pretty weird, but sometimes you can feel that way, you really can. I know, because that's how I felt one time when I did something stupid to this big praying mantis I used to keep in my room as a pet.

I called the praying mantis Goblin. I called him that because he was all green, same as the Green Goblin in *Spider-Man*. I found him on a tree in our backyard and I made a cage for him and everything. I used an old fish tank that wasn't any good for keeping fish in anymore because it had a crack right down one side. I put in sand and a couple of rocks and some branches for Goblin to climb on and I made a lid so he couldn't get out. It looked pretty good, like a proper cage in a zoo or something.

It was fun having Goblin in my room. But the best part was feeding him. I used to catch insects and moths and what I'd do sometimes was, I'd tie them on the end of a long piece of cotton. Then I'd jiggle them up and down in Goblin's tank to make him think they were still alive.

When Goblin saw them he'd twist his head around like some kind of big-eyed robot. Then he'd start rocking and creeping closer. When he got right up close, he'd grab the moths in the bendy part of his arm where all the spikes were and chomp into them. Dad made a joke about it once. He said his name was Goblin because he was always gobbling his food. I thought it was a pretty good joke. Mum didn't. She just groaned.

But one day I did a really dumb thing. I caught this moth, but before I gave it to Goblin, I sprayed it with fly spray. That sounds pretty bad, I know, but I wasn't trying to hurt him or anything. It was sort of an experiment. I just wanted to see what would happen. I never really thought he'd eat the stupid moth. But Goblin did eat it, all of it, and what happened was, he died.

I thought he was going to be all right. He looked okay when I went to bed. But in the morning when I checked the tank, he was lying on the sand with his stomach all eaten away and his legs and wings pulled off and a million black ants crawling all over him. If someone wanted to punch me that day, I would've let them.

So, all I'm saying is, maybe that's how my dad was feeling after he called Mister Mosely "just a dog." And maybe that's why he just stood there and let my mum punch him, even though he could have stopped her easily, seeing how he's way bigger and stronger than she is.

But it's still kind of weird my dad doing that, because what he said was true. Mister Mosely *was* just a dog. I mean it wasn't like he was a person or he could talk or anything. And he didn't have any special superpowers and he didn't go around rescuing people or catching bad guys the way that police dog on TV does. And I guess he wasn't the smartest dog in the world either, because he only ever learned one trick, even though it was a pretty good one.

So you see, Dad was only telling the truth when he said what he said. Didn't stop Mum from punching him, though. Maybe there are some things you shouldn't say, even if they are true.

Anyway, I'm just letting you know all that so you don't think these stories I'm writing are going to be about a superhero TV kind of dog. They're not. They're just going to be about a normal, everyday dog. Our dog, Mister Mosely. And they will all be true.

Even the ones that I wish weren't.

2

GETTING MISTER MOSELY

We got Mister Mosely because of Uncle Gavin. I was only about three then. Some stuff I can remember and some stuff I only know because Mum and Dad told me about it after. Sometimes I'm not too sure which is which because it was almost seven years ago now.

Uncle Gavin's my dad's brother. Dad used to call him his "little" brother, seeing how he's younger than Dad. But it was kind of a joke my dad calling him that, because Uncle Gavin is taller and bigger than him.

Whenever Uncle Gavin came over, Dad used to say, "How's it going, Little Brother?" and Uncle Gavin would say, "Not bad, B.B." B.B. stands for "Big

Brother." But I haven't heard Dad and Uncle Gavin do that for a long time, because Uncle Gavin doesn't come around to our place the way he used to, and we never go to his place anymore either.

I don't have a little brother or a big brother. I've got two little sisters instead. One's just a baby. They're all right most of the time, I guess. Their names are Amelia and Grace. And if you want to know, my name's Corey. Corey Ingram. But back when we got Mister Mosely, there wasn't any Amelia or Grace, just me and Mum and Dad.

Not for long, though, because Mum was pregnant. Dad took photos the day we went to Uncle Gavin's to get Mister Mosely and you can see Mum's belly sticking right out. Mum reckons she looks like she's swallowed a beach ball in those photos. I really wanted Mum to have a boy baby so then me and him could be big brother and little brother, same as Dad and Uncle Gavin, but it just ended up being Amelia.

Anyway, why we got Mister Mosely from Uncle Gavin was because he owned two dogs and they had all these puppies. Uncle Gavin's dogs were purebred

Dalmatians. They cost a lot of money, but that wouldn't worry Uncle Gavin because Mum reckons he's loaded. He's got his own business building stuff and he's the boss of everything. That's how come at Christmas, Uncle Gavin always gives the best presents. Once he bought Dad a big tool kit that Dad was saving up for ages to get, and he bought Mum some perfume that she said "cost the earth." I'm not sure if we'll get any presents from Uncle Gavin this year, though.

And just in case you don't know, Dalmatians are those big spotty dogs they had in that movie *101 Dalmatians*. Except Uncle Gavin didn't have that many. He only had two — a girl dog he called Madonna and a boy dog he called Prince. He named them after his favorite singers. They're both dead now. I mean the dogs, not the singers, except I'm not sure about the Prince guy.

Why Uncle Gavin bought Madonna and Prince in the first place was to breed them. Then he was going to sell the puppies or maybe put them in dog shows and win heaps of prizes and trophies. But it didn't work out that way, even though Madonna ended up having ten puppies. That was because all the puppies were "bitsers," which means they weren't real purebred Dalmatians like Madonna and Prince. They had "bits" of other kinds of dogs mixed up in them. Uncle Gavin wasn't happy about that, but Dad said it was his own fault.

The puppies were bitsers because Uncle Gavin forgot to lock the gate to the kennels one time and Madonna got out. So I guess that meant Prince didn't end up being the dad. When the puppies didn't come out proper Dalmatians, Uncle Gavin didn't want them anymore. He reckoned they were "no bloody use" to him and he was just going to give them all away. That's when he said to Mum and Dad that if they wanted one, they could have first pick.

I definitely remember when Mum and Dad told me we were getting a puppy. I couldn't believe it. It was even better than getting a brand-new brother or a brand-new sister. And the best part was, I got to pick the one I wanted — which definitely didn't happen with Amelia.

3

NAMING MISTER MOSELY

How Mister Mosely got his name is a bit of a weird story. It all started the day we went to Uncle Gavin's to choose our puppy.

Dad said the puppies were a real mixed bag. He was right. When we looked in the kennel, some were spotty, some were nearly all black or brown, some were pretty big, some were little, some had short hair, some were furry. There was even one that had really long ears, and it kept stepping on them and tripping over them, which was pretty funny. Only a couple of the puppies looked like proper Dalmatians to me, but Uncle Gavin said even they weren't really right.

When Uncle Gavin opened up the gate to the kennel, all the puppies came running out at us. I remember they started jumping up on me and licking and scratching my legs and trying to chew my shoes. Mum says she had to pick me up to stop me from crying. I don't remember that bit, but maybe it was true, seeing how I was only a little kid then.

The puppies didn't worry Dad at all. Uncle Gavin took a video that day. In the video, Dad's lying on the grass, letting them climb all over him and lick his face and bite his ears. Mum and me are laughing at him. Dad's laughing too, and you can hear him saying, "Help! Help! Save me! I'm being eaten alive by a pack of mad dogs!" He used to do stupid stuff like that once.

It must have been after Uncle Gavin stopped filming that I saw Mister Mosely for the very first time. He hadn't run out with the other puppies. He was back up at the kennel gate, sitting beside Madonna, just sort of watching and waiting. He looked all white and the sun made his coat go shiny.

I liked him right away. Maybe it was because he

was just sitting there kind of waiting for me to see him. Mum reckons I pointed straight at him and said, "I want that one."

Dad didn't think much of my pick. He told me I should choose a puppy with a bit more "get-up-and-go." He said my puppy looked a bit dopey and we should get a spotty puppy, one that was almost a true Dalmatian. He kept saying stuff like "You don't want that other one. He's no good. He's hardly got any spots. He's not like a real Dalmatian. He's mostly white."

But I did want him, and that's what I kept telling Dad.

"I do! I want that one! The *mostly* one!" That's what Mum and Dad reckoned I kept saying over and over. "I want the mostly one! I want the mostly one!"

The next bit I don't really remember exactly, but Mum says that Dad picked up my puppy and looked him right in the face and said, "Well, Mister *Mostly*, it looks like you're *it* — looks like you're the chosen one." Dad always joked that he gave in "just to shut me up."

Anyway, I guess it was because I heard Dad say it that I started to call the new puppy Mister Mostly too. Only problem was, I couldn't say it properly because I was just a little kid. I always left out the *t* bit so it came out Mister *Mosely*. And because I called him Mister Mosely that's what Mum and Dad started calling him too, except for sometimes when they called him Mister Moe or just plain Moe. Then Dad painted the name on the side of this big silver food bowl we bought, and he spelled it M-O-S-E-L-Y because he said "mose" rhymed with "hose."

So that's the story of how Mister Mosely got his name. Now I can't imagine him ever being called anything else. So I think it's pretty weird how it all happened just because he was "mostly" white.

4

MISTER MOSELY AS A PUPPY

I don't remember that much about Mister Mosely when he was just a puppy, probably because he didn't stay little for very long. I know he made heaps of puddles and messes on the floor, which Mum didn't like. That's how come we got the "no dogs inside" rule.

I do remember what happened on the first night we brought Mister Mosely home. Things didn't go too well. What happened was, Dad made this great place for Moe to sleep downstairs in the laundry room, but Mum didn't think it was such a good idea. She reckoned Mister Mosely was a real "people puppy" and he'd be too scared and lonely down there by himself.

She was right. Every time we left Mister Mosely alone, he went crazy with all this howling and whining.

That's why Dad tried this thing he'd read about. He got a big teddy bear I used to have when I was really little and an old windup clock that was his dad's and he put them both in with Mister Mosely. The bear was so Mister Mosely wouldn't feel alone, and the clock ticking was supposed to sound like a heart beating. Dad said it would make Moe think he was still with his mum, Madonna.

I thought Dad's idea was a pretty good one. Except it didn't work. When we left Mister Mosely in his bed with the teddy bear and the ticking clock, he just whined and carried on the same as before. Mum wanted to go straight back downstairs and get him, but Dad said we had to give his plan more time to work. So we stayed upstairs and waited.

We never did find out for sure if Dad's plan would've worked or not. That was because he forgot to turn the clock alarm off, and when Mister Mosely was in the laundry room all by himself, still whining and everything, it went *BRRRRRRIIIIIIIIIIING!*

It was really loud. Moe got such a fright he wee-ed all over the place and howled worse than ever.

After that, Mum said there was no way in the world we could leave Mister Mosely downstairs by himself, so Dad had to make a brand-new place for him. He made it on the porch at the top of the stairs just outside the back door. Dad said it was only a short-term measure, but it became Moe's spot from then on. That's where he always sat, waiting around for us to come outside or looking in on us like he was on guard or something.

I think the reason why Mister Mosely didn't stay little for long was because he ate so much. Mum used to joke that he was eating us out of house and home, and Dad reckoned he had "hollow legs," which meant that that's where all the food was going.

All I know is, Moe grew up way faster than me. I used to tie ropes to his collar and sit in a cardboard box and he could drag me across the grass no trouble at all. Sometimes I'd climb up on his back and pretend he was a horse. Mum made me stop doing that horse stuff. She said I might hurt him. I don't think he minded one bit. Nothing ever seemed to bother Moe, not even all that terrible stuff my little sister Amelia used to do to him.

That's another story I'm going to tell you about. But not now. First, I have to tell you what Mister Mosely looked like when he got to be a full-grown dog.

You couldn't miss him, that's for sure.

5

WHAT MISTER MOSELY LOOKED LIKE

First of all, Mister Mosely was big.

Not when we got him, though. He was smaller than a lot of the other puppies, but Uncle Gavin said that didn't mean he would stay small. "Big paws, big dog" — that's what Uncle Gavin reckoned, and Mister Mosely's paws were BIG all right.

They were so big, he used to get all tangled up in them. Sometimes Dad called him Un-co Moe when he did that, which was short for uncoordinated. I didn't think that was fair. I figured that Moe was just born with his adult dog feet and he had to wait for the rest of him to catch up.

He didn't have to wait too long. Moe got big extra fast. Pretty soon he was so big he had to put his front legs apart just so he could eat from his food bowl. One time when we went to the zoo, I saw a giraffe do the exact same thing. Dad ended up putting Moe's bowl on top of some blocks so he didn't have to bend all the way down to reach it. And we've got this photo of Moe standing on his back legs with his paws on Dad's chest, and Moe's head is as high as Dad's. That shows you how big he was.

Uncle Gavin said Mister Mosely must've had some other kind of really big dog in him. Maybe a Great Dane or a Rottweiler. Uncle Gavin called it "Moe's secret ingredient," just like in that recipe for fried chicken. He reckoned a lot of secret herbs and spices must have gone in to make Mister Mosely. Uncle Gavin always thought that was really funny.

The second thing you couldn't miss about Mister Mosely was his color, which, I already told you, was mostly white. Mr. Lafranchi from down the road called Moe the Unholy Ghost. That was because one night, when he was walking home really late, Moe came running out of the dark. Mr. Lafranchi said he almost had a heart attack because all he could see was a big white shape floating toward him. Mum said knowing where Mr. Lafranchi spent most of his evenings, it was a wonder he didn't see two Mister Moselys coming for him.

But the thing is, Moe wasn't pure white like a ghost is anyway. He had a few black bits on him too. The bits of Mister Mosely that were black were half of his left ear, his nose, some little dots you could hardly see on his back legs, a spot under his right eye that looked like a black tear coming out, and a few big black spots on his chest that all joined together and made a wonky heart shape. Mum said those spots on his chest were there because Mister Mosely's heart was too big for all of it to fit on the inside. The only other dark bits of Mister Mosely were his big round eyes. The rest of him was white.

That's why Mister Mosely didn't end up looking much like a proper Dalmatian at all. He was just too big and too white. And according to Uncle Gavin, Moe's fur was longer than it should've been and his head was too "dopey" and "boxy" and it didn't have the classic Dalmatian curves.

But I didn't care about any of that stuff. I liked

Mister Mosely just the way he was, and if I had to choose between him and a real Dalmatian — even one that cost a lot of money and won heaps of prizes and ribbons at stupid dog shows — I'd pick Mister Mosely every time. Same as I did when he was a puppy.

The only thing I hated Uncle Gavin saying was one time when he called Mister Mosely "Frankenstein's dog." He said that because he reckoned Moe was big and scary the way Frankenstein was and he said they'd both been thrown together from spare parts.

That was a stupid thing to say. Moe wasn't any kind of monster. Nobody who knew him properly was ever scared of him. Not even Amelia. Not even when she was so little, she had to stand on her toes and stretch right up just so she could pat him on the back and Moe could have swallowed her in about two gulps if he wanted to.

Amelia was never scared of Mister Mosely. But I reckon Mister Mosely definitely should have been scared of her.

6

MISTER MOSELY
AND AMELIA

My sister Amelia was always doing terrible stuff to Mister Mosely.

It started when she was little and she used to climb all over him and hold his ears up in the air and turn him into a "wabbit," or pull the skin out around his mouth and eyes just to make him look stupid.

It got worse when she was a bit bigger. That's when she started dressing him up. She made Moe wear all these wigs and dumb hats and scarves and she put big plastic earrings on him and decorated him with flowers and tinsel and all sorts of stuff. Moe always let Amelia do whatever she wanted. He just sat there and waited till she got bored or someone came and rescued him.

One of the worst things Amelia did was the day she found a packet of glitter in Mum's scrapbook drawer and covered Mister Mosely with it. Then she brought him in to show everyone how sparkly he looked. Wherever Moe went, he left a trail of glitter behind him, and before we could get him outside, he did one of those giant shakes he does after you give him a wash and all this glitter sprayed everywhere. Dad said it was better than the Sydney Harbour Bridge fireworks on New Year's Eve.

Mum wasn't happy at all about the glitter going everywhere, but Amelia told her it was fairy dust and that Mister Mosely was a magic fairy dog and he was spreading his "good-luck doggie magic" all around the world.

But it wasn't very good luck for Mum and Dad and me. They had to clean up all the mess inside and I had to give Mister Mosely a bath to try to get the glitter off him. That wasn't easy. Even after two washes, he still sparkled a bit. So did I, on account of halfway through his first wash, he did another one of his giant shakes and I got totally soaked.

But the glitter wasn't the worst thing Amelia ever did to Mister Mosely. What she did with the marking pens was way worse. What happened was, one day when no one was looking, Amelia got some thick marking pens and drew all over Mister Mosely with them. She drew big round black glasses and bushy red eyebrows and a weird-looking mustache and some spiky hair on top of his head. Then she tried to draw a tie and collar around his neck, but they didn't turn out too good.

We only found out what Amelia did when she came and said she had a big surprise to show us. Then she made us all come downstairs, and she brought Mister Moe out from under the house and said, "Ta-daaaa!" like she'd done some kind of magic act or something.

Mum and Dad tried to go cross on her, but when they looked at Mister Mosely's face, they both started laughing and then they couldn't stop. They laughed so much they had tears coming out of their eyes and Mum had to run to the bathroom because she said she was going to be sick. Every time she tried to come back, Mister Mosely just had to look at her and make his drawn-on eyebrows go up in the air and Mum would run away again, holding her stomach. She laughed so much, one time I think I heard her make a little fart noise, and I didn't think Mum even did that kind of stuff.

Moe had no clue what was going on that day. He just stood there wagging his tail and half barking, half whining at us, trying to figure it out. He probably thought everyone had gone crazy. Then Dad got a mirror and held it up so he could see what Amelia had done to him. When Moe saw himself in the mirror, his ears and his new bushy eyebrows stuck up in the air. Then he twisted his head around one way and then the other, like he couldn't work out what he was looking at. That made Mum go tearing off to the bathroom again.

It was only after I gave Mister Mosely a bath to clean him up that we found out the pen Amelia used for Moe's red eyebrows was a permanent ink one.

After his first wash, when the eyebrows didn't come off, Mum said, "Poor old Moe — what has she done to you?" Then she got *another* fit of the giggles.

It took a long time and lots of washes and scrubbing for those eyebrows to come totally off, so Mister Mosely went around for ages looking really surprised all the time.

It was bad what Amelia did, drawing all that stuff on Mister Mosely, but she was only little and I guess it didn't really hurt Moe at all. Besides, it was sort of good too because of how it made Mum and Dad laugh so much they cried. Afterward, Amelia said she was sorry and Mum made her promise not to do anything like that again. But Dad said if we ever needed any extra money, we could always rent Mister Mosely out as a whiteboard.

Mum gave Dad a punch on the arm for that. Just a pretend one, though.

7

MISTER MOSELY AND STRANGERS

Mister Mosely didn't ever scare Amelia, but he did scare some people, even if he didn't mean to.

Like there was this one time when I was pretty little and we all went to a big fair thing down in the park. There were lots of stalls and rides and stuff and heaps and heaps of people. We took Mister Mosely along too because there was a dog competition. Moe won two prizes, one for Biggest Dog and one for Friendliest Dog. That just shows how people shouldn't have been afraid of him. Sometimes they were, though, and there were two people at the fair that day who Moe really scared.

It all started when I got lost in the crowd. Mum was taking Amelia to the toilets and Dad was talking to someone about Mister Mosely. I was supposed to "stay close and not wander off," but I went to have a look at this donkey that was taking kids for rides. I followed it around for a while without really thinking and then I couldn't find my way back. I must have headed off the wrong way, because I ended up at some part of the park I hadn't even seen before.

When I couldn't find Mum and Dad anywhere, I got really worried. It was getting dark and some people were starting to pack up to go home. I thought maybe I'd been left behind and I might have to sleep in the park all night. Pretty stupid, I know, but that's what I thought. I remember I cried a little bit. I couldn't help it. Then this man and lady found me.

I told them how I was lost and they said I could come with them. They gave me something to drink and some fries, which made me feel a lot better. Their car was parked on the road near where we were and they said there was a police station right around the corner and they would drive me there and then the police would phone Mum and Dad up and they'd come and get me. They said I should hurry up and go with them straightaway, because

Mum and Dad would be really worried about me. They seemed nice, so that's what I did.

Their car was a pretty bomby-looking one, though. The lady got in the front to drive and the man said he would sit with me in the back so I wouldn't be alone. He had a blanket there too in case I got cold. He opened the door for me to get in and that's what I was going to do when I heard Mister Mosely barking. I knew it was him straight-away because his bark was so deep and he sort of howled a bit when he barked too.

It took me a while to spot Moe because there were still plenty of people walking about everywhere. Then I saw him and Dad. They were right across the other side of the park, so I shouted out at them as loud as I could. Dad didn't hear me because I could see him still looking around everywhere trying to find me. But Moe heard me all right, and as soon as he did, he yanked the lead from Dad's hand and came charging across the park, swerving his way in between all the people and nearly knocking some of them over.

I was really happy to see Moe charging at me

that day and I could tell he was really happy to see me too. But I guess the man and the lady didn't know Moe was just being happy. I guess he must have looked pretty scary to them with his white face and his dark eyes and him being so big and running full speed straight at them and barking and howling, with his mouth flopping around everywhere.

Anyway, before I could tell them it was just old Moe happy to see me, the man jumped into the car and slammed the door shut and wound up the window. Then the lady drove off so fast the tires spun around and dust and dirt went everywhere. They were already gone when Moe got there, so he just barked a bit at the car when it went down the road and then he licked me half to death.

When Dad found us, he was pretty cross at me for not staying where I was supposed to, so I didn't tell him about the man and the lady. I figured he wouldn't like me talking to strangers and I knew he definitely wouldn't be happy if he found out I was going to get into their car.

The end of this story is that after, when we were driving away from the park, I asked Mum where the police station was and she said there wasn't one. She said the nearest one was miles away in the next suburb.

I didn't ask any more questions after that. I just sat in the backseat and held on to Mister Mosely all the way home.

8

THINGS THAT SCARED
MISTER MOSELY

I guess Mister Mosely frightened some people because he was so big and maybe kind of scary-looking. But there were lots of things that frightened *him* too.

Way back when he wasn't fully grown, the first thing that scared him was thunder. One night we had this big storm. It started with just a bit of lightning and stuff. Mister Mosely was out on the porch and he was already shaking and whining a bit. Then a big boom came. I thought a plane or something had crashed onto the roof.

Anyway, Mister Moe forgot all about Mum's "no dogs inside" rule and bolted straight in through the back door. He was going really fast, and when he tried to stop, his feet skidded all over the place like he was a cartoon dog. Then he ran into my room and hid under my bed. He was shaking so much and he looked so scared that Mum said he could stay there "just this once," until the storm was over.

I guess Mum forgot about the "just this once" bit because after that, whenever there was a storm with even a tiny bit of thunder, Mister Mosely ran inside. And it was always my bed he hid under. When he got bigger, he had to squeeze himself flat just to fit, and the bed would lift up on one side. I don't think we could have got him out then even if we'd wanted to.

When I was little and Mister Mosely was under my bed, I used to crawl under with him, especially when there was a bad storm and the thunder got really loud, like someone setting off bombs. I'd pretend we were hiding in a cave together.

I liked being under the bed with Moe. I used to put my head on his chest and listen to him breathing and his heart beating. He was so big and strong

I didn't think any storm would ever be bad enough to blow him away. I just held on to Moe's neck and I felt safe. The first time Mum and Dad found me like that, I told them I was looking after Mister Mosely so he wouldn't be too frightened. I guess they probably knew it was really the other way around.

But it wasn't just thunder that frightened Mister Mosely. Dad's electric leaf blower was another thing he hated. He hated it so much he wouldn't go near it, even when it was turned off. All you had to do was pretend you were going to pick it up and Moe would run away with his tail between his legs. One day, just as a joke, Dad started saying, "Leeeaf blower. Leeeaf blower. I'm going to get the leeeaf blower," in a sort of slow and scary way and Mister Mosely got the shakes. Mum reckoned it was cruel and made Dad stop, but I could tell she was trying not to laugh because Moe looked so funny.

Even Tiger scared Mister Mosely. Tiger was the skinny cat from next door that didn't even come halfway up one of Moe's legs. Tiger belonged to the Contis. They called it Tiger because it had orange stripes. Tiger was a she, and the weird thing about her was she was totally deaf.

Mister Mosely wasn't always scared of Tiger. But one day when she was in our yard, just licking her paws, Mister Mosely came up behind her and sniffed her. I guess Tiger didn't hear Moe coming on account of her being deaf, because she got this giant fright and sort of frizzed up and shot straight into the air like she'd stepped on a landmine or something. When she was still in the air, Tiger twisted around and turned into some kind of a ninja cat and started hissing and whacking into Mister Mosely's face with her claws.

If Moe almost gave Tiger a heart attack when he came up behind her, I reckon Tiger gave Moe a triple heart attack. After that, whenever Tiger came into our backyard, Mister Mosely would tear up the back stairs and bark at her from the porch. It didn't bother Tiger, though, because she couldn't hear a thing. She just walked around our yard as calm as anything. It drove poor old Moe nuts.

One day Uncle Gavin was over at our place and Mister Mosely started barking at Tiger from the top of the stairs. When he saw Moe up there hiding from Tiger, Uncle Gavin called him a chicken and said he needed to "fire up more." Uncle Gavin was always saying things like that about Moe and always trying to make him angry by teasing him and roughing him up and boxing him around the head a bit. It never worked. Moe just used to wag his tail and wait for Uncle Gavin to get tired of it and give up, same as he did with Amelia.

It made me angry when Uncle Gavin did that kind of stuff. If Mum or Dad was there, they made him stop, but if it was just me, Uncle Gavin would keep doing it. Sometimes I used to wish that Mister Moe *would* fire up and really teach Uncle Gavin a lesson, but he never did. He always just waited till it was over. Mister Mosely was good at waiting. Mum said he had "the patience of Job." Job was some guy from the Bible who had heaps of patience. At least that's what Mum told me.

There was only one time I can remember when Mister Mosely ever got really angry with someone. On that day, he was so fired up it was scary. But it wasn't at Uncle Gavin. I'll tell you all about that soon, but first I have to tell you about the thing that scared Mister Mosely the most, even more than thunder or the leaf blower or Tiger.

I have to tell you about the Pink Panther.

9

MISTER MOSELY AND THE PINK PANTHER

Dad got the Pink Panther for Mum way back before they were even married. It's this giant stuffed toy that's almost as big as a person and looks just like the Pink Panther in all those cartoons. We call him Pinkie for short.

Just about every Christmas, Dad would tell the story of how he got Pinkie for Mum. What happened was, Dad took Mum to this fair thing and the Pink Panther was the big prize at the Knock 'em Down stall. Mum loved the Pink Panther as soon as she saw it, so Dad really wanted to win it for her. All he had to do was throw some balls and knock down a pile of wooden blocks.

Dad played heaps of cricket, so it should have been easy, but he reckoned the whole thing was rigged. He said the balls were all light and wobbly and out of shape and some of the blocks must have weighed a ton or been nailed down because he said he hit them, but they didn't move. Dad spent all his money trying to win the top prize for Mum, but he couldn't do it. Mum wanted him to stop because she was worried about him losing all his money, but he kept going. Mum says that just shows Dad's stubborn streak.

Anyway, Dad ran out of money so Mum didn't get her prize, but the next time they went out, Dad told Mum he'd hired a chauffeur for the night. Mum didn't know what he was talking about. But when she looked in the front seat of Dad's car, she saw the Pink Panther sitting there like he was the driver. Dad had sticky-taped his paws to the wheel and put one of those driver's caps on his head.

How Dad got the Pink Panther was, he borrowed some money from his boss and he went back to the fair the next day and just bought it. He never told

Mum how much it cost him, but he said he had to do a "mountain" of overtime to pay his boss back. Dad reckoned it was worth it. He said that the Pink Panther earned him lots of brownie points.

So that's how come we had the Pink Panther at our place. I thought he was pretty cool because he was so big, but Mister Mosely didn't think he was cool at all. He wouldn't go anywhere near him. And you could tell Moe was really scared, because when he barked at Pinkie, he was always shaking so much that the bark came out all wobbly, like someone was strangling him at the same time.

Mum blamed Dad. She said Mister Mosely probably had an inbuilt fear of stuffed toys after that teddy-bear-alarm-clock thing when Moe was a puppy. I just think Mister Mosely thought the Pink Panther was some kind of scary-looking person.

Most of the time, the Pink Panther didn't worry Moe, because he was locked away in the cupboard. But at Christmas we brought him out and dressed him up as Santa Claus. We used to sit him on a chair next to the Christmas tree in the living room. Mister Mosely could see him from the back door.

He'd just stare and stare at Pinkie. I think Moe was terrified he was going to move.

One Christmas the Pink Panther did move. Sort of. It was when Uncle Gavin was over at our house and he snuck around behind the armchair so Moe couldn't see him. Then he got in behind Pinkie and lifted up his arms and made it look like he was getting up from the seat. When Mister Mosely saw Pinkie moving, he almost killed himself trying to get away down the stairs.

Uncle Gavin almost killed himself too, only with laughing. After that, we had to hide Pinkie in the next room where Moe couldn't see him, otherwise he wouldn't come back on the porch. Mum wasn't very happy with Uncle Gavin.

We had to stop dressing Pinkie up as Santa because of the thing that happened a couple of Christmases ago.

10

MISTER MOSELY'S
WHITE CHRISTMAS

One Christmas, all of us were in the living room watching TV, and Pinkie was sitting in his usual place next to the tree. Amelia was playing with some toys on the floor just in front of him. While she was playing, she must have bumped into Pinkie's chair or something because he toppled off it and fell right on her. Amelia got a fright when that happened and sort of squealed.

Mister Mosely must have been watching everything from the back door, because as soon as Pinkie landed on top of Amelia, he came charging into the living room. I guess he thought she was being attacked or something, because before we could stop him, Moe grabbed Pinkie by the throat and dragged him away. Then he started shaking him so hard that Pinkie ripped all the way down one side and his head almost tore right off.

Everyone was shouting and yelling at Moe to stop, but he just kept shaking Pinkie like crazy until millions of those little white Styrofoam balls started pouring out of him and they got blown all around the room because the ceiling fan was going full blast. Dad tried grabbing Pinkie from Moe but he wouldn't let go, and they had a kind of tug-of-war for a while. Moe won, because the leg Dad was holding on to ripped right off and he went crashing to the floor.

When Mister Mosely finally realized that Pinkie wasn't fighting back, he just stood there. You could tell he knew he'd done something bad, because he let Pinkie drop out of his mouth and put his head way down near the floor and his big eyes started looking around at us, all worried. His tail started wagging too, but only a tiny bit.

Then the little white balls that were flying around everywhere began sticking to Mister Mosely's nose and that made him sneeze. Then he sneezed again.

And again. We were being spattered with spit and snot. I had to help Dad drag Moe outside before we all got drowned.

It took forever to clean up all those little Styrofoam balls. They were everywhere, all over the carpet and in between the couch cushions and in the light shades and in our hair and on our clothes. Even the Christmas tree was covered in them. Dad called it Moe's White Christmas.

No one was really too mad at Mister Mosely for tearing up Pinkie. Mum even called him Amelia's knight in furry white armor because of how he came to rescue her. One time, Dad told me you were only brave when something scared you but you faced up to it anyway. He told me that when I didn't want to swim the whole length of the pool at school and some kids at school called me a chicken. So maybe Mum was right and maybe Mister Mosely was brave when he saved Amelia from the Pink Panther, even though she wasn't really being attacked in the first place.

Anyway, Mum bought all this new stuffing for Pinkie and she sewed him back together, but every time we tried to put him back on the chair, Mister Mosely went crazy. Even if we closed the screen door, he just kept barking and scratching at it and banging his head against it, trying to get inside. So that's how come we had to put the Pink Panther back in the cupboard for good.

I don't really care that much about Pinkie being locked away — except it meant that Dad stopped telling the story of how he got him for Mum. But maybe it wouldn't have made any difference anyway because pretty soon Dad stopped telling all his other stories too.

When he did talk, it was only about work and money and bills and stuff.

11

THE WEIRDEST MISTER
MOSELY STORY

That time Mister Mosely ripped up the Pink Panther was pretty weird, but it isn't the weirdest story about Mister Mosely. That happened one morning when I found him next door in Mr. Taylor's yard.

That was the first weird thing, because Mister Mosely never went next door, even though there's this big hole in the fence where a couple of palings are broken off. He was acting kind of weird too. He was just wandering around near the old shed in Mr. Taylor's backyard like he couldn't make up his mind where to go.

I was up on our back porch when I saw him, so I called out to him. That's when it got even weirder. Moe started to come home, but something really strange happened when he got about halfway across Mr. Taylor's yard. All of a sudden, he just sort of stopped dead and jerked back around and wouldn't come any farther. I thought maybe he heard a noise behind him or something, but he just stood there whining for a bit, and then he went back to the shed.

I knew something was wrong with him, because Moe always came when I called him. So I tried again, but the exact same thing happened. He got halfway across the yard and wouldn't come any farther. Even when I clapped my hands and shouted at him, it didn't make any difference. There was something in the middle of the yard that was stopping him, like an invisible wall or one of those force fields they have in *Star Trek*. I kept calling and calling him, but he did the same thing every time.

Then Dad came out to see what all the racket was about. When I told him what was happening, he did his really loud whistle thing that I wish I could do, and he shouted out to Mister Mosely in his serious, "I'm not mucking around" voice.

But the same thing happened for Dad that happened for me. Except this time, when Moe started to come home, he was going a bit slower and his head was hanging way down near the grass. When he got to that same spot his head just twisted slowly around and he stayed there making that whiny kind of noise he makes when something is really upsetting him.

"What's wrong with him?"

That's what my dad said. I just shook my head because I didn't have a clue. Dad said we'd better go and check him out, and that's what we did. Dad climbed over the fence first, then he lifted me over. I knew something was definitely wrong when we got into Mr. Taylor's yard because I really thought Mister Mosely would come running over to meet us, but he didn't. All he did was wag his tail a bit and stay where he was. I just kept thinking, *What's going on?*

It was Dad who saw it first. I only saw it when I got right up close to where Moe was standing. There was something like string coming out of his mouth. Only it wasn't string, it was fishing line, and it went from out the side of Moe's mouth right across the yard and into Mr. Taylor's shed. We couldn't see it at all from back in our yard because it was so thin and clear.

Dad told me to hold Mister Mosely to quieten him down and keep him still. Then he got Mister Mosely by the head so he could open up his mouth. Old Moe wasn't too happy about that. He was watching Dad and breathing really fast and whining at him. You could tell he was scared, but he let Dad open his mouth anyway.

That's when we saw the big fishhook. It was stuck right in the side of Mister Mosely's gum. Dad told me to go and see where the other end of the fishing line went. I was pretty happy to do that, because looking at the fishhook in Moe's gum made me feel a bit sick in the stomach.

I went into the shed and found that the other end of the line was on a fishing rod that was lying on the floor. It was caught in the doorway. What Dad and me worked out was that the hook probably had some old bait still on it, because Mr. Taylor was retired and he went fishing all the time. Moe must have smelled the bait and tried to eat it and got himself hooked just like a fish would. Then when he tried to come back home, he must have pulled the fishing rod over and it got stuck in the doorway.

And that's why Mister Mosely always stopped half-way across the yard, because the fishing line was pulling tight on the reel and yanking the hook even deeper into his gum.

"Poor old fella," Dad said.

Mister Mosely looked up at both of us. His big dark eyes were jumping around everywhere and he was making a really high whiny sound. It was the same sound he made whenever he did something wrong. The spot under his eye really could have been a big black tear that day. All I could think of was how many times I called poor Moe to come home, and how he kept trying to come, even though he knew it was going to hurt him every time.

Anyway, what happened then was, Dad said that the hook was in too deep for him to get out, so he cut the fishing line with his pocketknife, and we drove Mister Mosely to the vet. Like I said, it was one of the weirdest days ever.

But it wasn't over yet.

12

MISTER MOSELY
AT THE VET'S

The vet we took Mister Mosely to when he got the fishhook stuck in his gum was a lady vet. She kept saying how beautiful Moe was and she called him Big Boy all the time. I liked her a lot.

When we got there, she took us into this special room and asked Dad and me to hold on to Mister Mosely while she tried to get the hook out. She said a dog with a fishhook stuck in his gum was a first for her. Moe was really scared. I could tell because he kept whining and licking me and putting his head down low, which is what he always did when he was frightened or worried. I was a bit scared too, because I wasn't sure what was going to happen.

The first thing the vet did was give Mister Mosely a needle in his jaw right near the hook so he wouldn't feel any pain. He jumped a bit when she did that, and Dad and me had to hold on tight so he wouldn't run away. Then she got out some sort of pliers to pull the hook out. They looked just the same as the ones in Dad's toolbox.

At the beginning, I wanted to watch everything the vet was doing because it was pretty cool, like seeing a real operation up close, which I'd never done before. But after a while I didn't feel too good. I think it was because of all the bad smells in the room — the weird medicine smells and the farty smells coming from Mister Mosely, who couldn't help it because he was just so frightened.

As soon as the vet started grabbing on to the hook with those plier things, I started to feel really bad. I was trying not to look at the blood in Moe's mouth or the blood on the rubber gloves the vet was wearing. Then the vet gave up on the pliers because they weren't working, and she went to the table where all her vet stuff was. When she came back, she had a really pointy, sharp-looking knife in her hand.

Straightaway, I started to go all cold and sweaty. It felt like something had sucked all the blood from my head and some big blob was rolling around in my stomach. The vet told me I looked as pale as a sheet and she thought maybe I should go outside and get some fresh air and a glass of water. I thought so too, so that's what I did.

When I got to the girl at the front desk, I tried to ask her for some water, but I didn't really get to finish asking because my head went all heavy and swirly like when you go upside down in a roller coaster loop. Then I passed out. I remember starting to fall and then I remember hearing a bell ringing. Then nothing. When I woke up, Dad was looking down at me, and he was holding something cold and wet on my head. It turned out to be a wet hankie.

The receptionist girl told me that I fainted right on top of her desk, and my head hit the little bell that you ring to let someone know you're there, which is kind of funny, I guess, as long as you're not the person fainting and hitting your head. I ended up with this big bruise on my cheek just under my eye, and the vet had to put a bandage around the cut on my forehead from the bell to stop it bleeding all over the place.

After that, I just lay down on the bench in the reception area, and Dad and the vet went back to try and fix Mister Mosely up. They were gone a while. When they came back, Moe was with them and he had these black, spiky stitches in his gum where the vet had to cut the hook out, and a plastic bucket thing tied around his neck to stop him from scratching at the stitches with his paws. He looked like a half dog, half vacuum cleaner, especially when he sniffed along the ground. It probably would have made me laugh if I didn't think I was going to throw up any second.

When it was time to leave the vet's, Dad had to carry me to the car because he was worried I was going to faint or vomit or both. He had to carry Mister Mosely too. That was because Moe couldn't see where he was going too well with his bucket helmet and he kept bumping into everything. The gas the vet gave him for the operation made him a bit wobbly too. Luckily, Dad was pretty strong, because not many people could pick Mister Mosely up. The only other person I ever saw do it was Uncle Gavin when he was showing off one time.

Dad said me and Mister Mosely were two peas in a pod that day. I guess that was pretty right, because neither of us could walk properly and we both had stuff on our heads, and even the bruise on my cheek matched that black tear spot thing under Mister Mosely's eye. It was even on the same side.

So like I said, I reckon that's the weirdest Mister Mosely story ever. Dad used to love telling it. Once he called it "the day Moe thought he was a fish," and he said Uncle Gavin must have got it wrong about Moe's secret ingredient. It wasn't Rottweiler or Great Dane at all. Dad reckoned it was grouper.

I loved it when Dad told that story. He made it sound so funny and it always made me laugh. Except maybe for the bit where Mister Mosely has the hook in his mouth and I keep calling him to come home and he keeps trying to come every time, even though he knows he can't. That bit's never funny.

13

MISTER MOSELY'S ONE TRICK

Some dogs can do heaps of tricks, like those circus dogs or the ones in the movies, but Mister Mosely only ever learned one trick. It was a pretty good one, though, and it just sort of happened by accident.

It all started because of the paper man. He drives an old VW with the top cut off. It sounds like a lawn mower and you can hear it coming from way down the road. The paper man chucks the newspapers from his car. He's a pretty good shot too, because he doesn't slow down too much and he hardly ever misses. He can land our paper right on the front lawn.

One time, when I was out the front getting the

mail for Mum, I heard the paper man's car coming down our street, so I waited for him. When he threw the paper into our yard, I tried to catch it before it hit the ground. I almost got it too, but it was spinning a lot and it hit my hands and bounced out.

After that, I wanted to see if I could catch the paper, so I started listening for the paper man. Most of the time I'd be mucking around with Mister Mosely in the backyard after school when we'd hear him coming. Then me and Mister Mosely would run around to the front of the house and I'd be trying to catch the paper and Moe would be jumping around trying to get it too. It was a lot of fun.

The very first time I caught a paper, the paper man tooted his horn and gave me the thumbs-up. I felt pretty good about that. It was like we were a team or something. My record ended up being five catches in a row without the paper hitting the ground once.

But there was one little problem. If I missed the paper and it did hit the ground, Mister Mosely would try to knock me out of the way and beat me to it. A few times I ended up doing a somersault across the grass. Moe wasn't trying to hurt me or anything — it was just a game to him and he didn't know how big and strong he was.

But the real problem was, if he got to the paper first, he'd be so excited he'd run off with it and slobber all over it. Sometimes he'd rip it up a bit before I could get it away from him. Moe didn't really understand the whole reading thing. But Dad wasn't too happy. So I had to teach Mister Mosely not to wreck the paper if he got it before me.

The first thing I taught him was not to run off with it, but just to pick it up and bring it to me and drop it at my feet. That took a while. Lucky for me, the paper was wrapped in plastic, so as long as Moe didn't chew it up too much or go crazy with it, none of his slobber got on the actual pages. Next I taught him to carry it in his mouth while I walked along beside him. Later on, he learned to bring it all the way around the house and up the back steps and drop it on the porch.

But one day something happened that I didn't expect. Just before the time the paper man normally came, Mum called me upstairs to tidy my room, which she reckoned was a pigsty, even though it really wasn't that bad. When I finished doing that, I went back out the front, but Mister Mosely wasn't there anymore. I hadn't heard the paper man come, but when I checked the back porch, there was Moe, wagging his tail at a million miles an hour with the newspaper in his mouth. He'd brought it up all by himself. I thought that was pretty good, so I gave him one of his favorite biscuits as a reward.

The next day I tested Moe to see if he would do it again. I stayed inside this time while he sat in his usual place on the porch. He must have heard the newspapers hitting the ground down the street or the sound of the paper man's car before me, because all of a sudden his ears stuck out like wings. Then he tore off down the stairs.

Pretty soon he was back at the screen door, whining and wagging his tail with the paper in his mouth. I gave him two biscuits that time. Dad always reckoned Mister Mosely wasn't "the sharpest tool in the shed." That meant he didn't think he was too smart. But when I showed him what Moe could do, he was pretty impressed. He said, "Maybe the old Moe's been holding out on us. Got a few brains after all, big fella."

Dad changed his mind about that after what happened on Saturday.

I don't really think it was all Mister Mosely's fault. The thing was, the Saturday paper didn't get delivered in the afternoon. It came really early in the morning. Anyway, when Dad got up and went to get the paper to read in bed with Mum like he always did, it wasn't there. Then he remembered Mister Mosely and his new trick, so he went to check the back porch to see if Moe had already brought it up. Moe had the paper all right. But he had eight other newspapers as well.

Dad got pretty angry at Mister Mosely, mainly because not everyone got their paper delivered and he had to go all around the neighborhood trying to find out who was missing one. I heard him say, "Definitely not the sharpest tool in the shed!" as he went off with all the papers tucked under his arm.

I don't think Dad was being very fair. I know Mister Mosely made a mistake and everything, but he didn't do what he did because he was dumb. I reckon he did it because he was smart. He must've figured if he got two biscuits for one paper, then the more papers he brought up, the more biscuits he'd get, which is pretty clever if you think about it. And the other reason why I reckon Mister Mosely was smart was because after Dad got mad at him that morning for fetching other people's papers, he never did it again. Not even once.

I quit waiting out front for the paper man or trying to catch the paper in the air or beat Moe to it, because fetching the paper became his special trick. He did it every day and he never forgot once. Mister Mosely loved fetching the paper so much, I reckon he would have kept on doing it even if he didn't get two of his favorite biscuits every time.

In the end, it took something even bigger than Moe to stop him.

14

MISTER MOSELY'S LOST FORTNIGHT

One of the worst days ever was the day Mister Mosely just disappeared. He was there in the afternoon, because I played with him after school, but at night when I took his big silver bowl out to feed him, he was gone. And he was still gone the next day.

Dad and me checked all the places he could be hiding, like under the garage, but he wasn't anywhere. Then we went around asking all the people on our street if they'd seen him. Everyone said no except for Mrs. Jarman down the road, who said she thought she saw a big white dog going past her house in the middle of the night when she got up to go to the toilet. But then she said she couldn't be sure, seeing as how it was dark and she didn't have her glasses on and maybe she imagined it anyway because she was half-asleep, so that didn't really help that much.

We drove all around the streets looking for Mister Mosely. Whenever we saw someone, we asked them about him and we'd describe him and everything, but no one was any help at all. I started to get really scared. I was thinking that maybe something bad had happened to him, like he'd been run over by a car and he was hurt somewhere or even worse. Mum and Dad kept saying that he would turn up any minute and they said not to worry, but I could tell that they were probably thinking the same thing as me.

The next day, when Dad went to work, Mum and me made little posters on the computer and printed them off. We put a picture of Mister Mosely on them, and at the top we had LOST — HAVE YOU SEEN OUR DOG? Underneath the picture, we put Mister Mosely's name and how he was big and just about all white and how he was friendly and wouldn't hurt anyone and our telephone number and e-mail address.

I wanted to put BIG REWARD! in capital letters too, but Mum said we couldn't afford to do that because Dad was really worried about losing his job at the electrical store on account of some recession thing. Mum told me that people would help us anyway, even if we didn't give them money. I was really hoping she was right.

We put the posters in people's mailboxes and on telephone poles and in shops and on the big notice board at the supermarket. But it didn't work. Only one person ever phoned us up and that was two days later. They told us that there was a white dog in the park across the road from their house. It was a long way away, but Mum and me got in the car and went straight there. When we got to the park, the dog was only about half as big as Mister Mosely and the people who owned it were right there having a picnic. It was just a big waste of time. It made me feel worse than ever because I thought we'd found him.

Mister Mosely was gone nearly two weeks and I didn't think we were ever going to get him back. It was so bad. Dad couldn't believe how a dog as big as Mister Mosely could just disappear. Me either. Sometimes I'd forget Moe was gone for a second and I'd go outside to play with him or I'd start to get some food out for him. Then I'd remember. I had to stop myself from crying when those kinds of things happened.

But then one night, when we were having tea, we heard all this scratching and whining coming from the back door. When we looked, Mister Mosely was standing there on the porch, wagging his tail like crazy. None of us could believe it.

Mum and Dad and Amelia and me ran over and just went mad patting and hugging him. Dad reckoned Mister Mosely was "back from the dead." We were all laughing and asking Moe where he'd been, even though there was no way he could tell us. He didn't care. He just kept on licking all our faces and whipping us with his tail and we just kept on talking and laughing and joking together.

If I had a special superpower or something and I could do time travel, that would be one time I'd go back to for sure. It was one of the best days ever. And that's not even the end of the story, because when Mister Mosely came home that night, we found out he'd brought some things back with him.

15

MISTER MOSELY'S MYSTERY

Mister Mosely looked just the same when he came home after being gone all that time, but there were two things different about him.

One was that he had three little red flowers stuck in the holes of his collar. They were made of plastic. Dad said they were poppies. The second thing was tied to his name tag. I was the one who spotted it first. It was a shiny ring with jewels on it. They were all different colors. Mum said they wouldn't be real jewels, just glass.

We couldn't figure out what the flowers and the fake ring were all about and we couldn't figure out where Mister Mosely had got to. First we thought maybe he'd been sick or hurt and someone had been taking care of him, but when we checked him over, he didn't have any cuts or marks on him or anything. And Mum reckoned Moe hadn't lost any weight either and he was as healthy as ever.

Dad said he'd read these stories about dogs being kidnapped and taken hundreds of miles away from where they lived, then escaping somehow and finding their way back home. But that couldn't have happened with Mister Mosely because his feet would have been all cut up and wrecked and they were the same as when he left.

Dad's other idea was that maybe he'd gone off with a female dog and maybe they had puppies somewhere. Mum didn't think that was right. She said if that was true, Mister Mosely still would have come home sometimes, and if there were puppies, he would still be going back there, which he wasn't. "Moe'd never run out on anyone," Mum reckoned.

In the end Dad said, "Maybe he just got sick of our ugly mugs and decided to try another family for a while — one that could give him a decent feed of caviar and steak every day." We all laughed, because at least we knew *that* wasn't true.

It drove me nuts not knowing where Mister Mosely had gone. Mum called it "Moe's lost fortnight." I used to make up stupid stories about it, mostly when I was lying in bed at night. Stories like how Moe was captured by a gang of crooks but escaped and then went and got the police to arrest them. Or how he discovered a secret terrorist plot and had to stop it. Or how aliens zapped him up but he outsmarted them and found his way back to Earth somehow. Or how he was really a secret agent dog and he'd been away working undercover on a top secret spy mission. I know all those stories are pretty stupid, because Mister Mosely was just a normal dog and couldn't have done any of those things. But I still liked making them up anyway.

If you really want to know what I think happened to Mister Mosely, I'll tell you. I think he was helping someone somehow. Like maybe there was somebody who needed him for those two weeks more than we did and that's why he stayed away. Maybe someone who was hurt or sick or someone who'd lost their memory or was in some kind of trouble. I can't say for sure if that's right or not, but I hope so. It's the kind of thing I think Moe would do.

In the end I guess it didn't really matter why Mister Mosely went away that time. It only mattered that he came back.

But I still haven't told you the best part of the Mister Mosely's Mystery story. The best part is how Mum took that ring I found on Moe's name tag to a jewelry shop just in case and found out that it wasn't a fake at all. The jewelry shop man said it was made of real pure white gold and it had real diamonds and rubies and sapphires in it. It was worth a lot of money. Dad wanted to keep it because we really needed the money on account of how his work was being cut back. But Mum said we couldn't because it didn't belong to us and it wouldn't be right. Mum won. She took the ring to the police and told them all about how Moe brought it home.

Then one day, when we'd forgotten all about it, the police rang Mum and told her that nobody had come to get the ring, so it was hers. We all went crazy when we heard that. Mum ended up selling it to the jeweler. She said the money was a godsend.

She said, without it, we would have lost our house for sure. That was because Dad had lost his job selling TVs and stuff and he still hadn't found a new one. Mum called Mister Mosely our guardian angel. She said he was definitely looking after us.

We never did find out where Moe went to that time. That's why I called this story Mister Mosely's Mystery. It's one of the worst Mister Mosely stories because of how bad it was when we thought he was gone for good. But it's one of the best ones too because of how Moe came home and because of the ring and everything.

Some stories are like that.

16

MY FAVORITE MISTER MOSELY STORY

One of the best things about Mister Mosely was how he used to wait out front of our house every day for me to come home from school.

He started doing that when I was nine. That's when Mum stopped picking me up from school because she had to work at the supermarket while Dad was trying to find another job. I didn't mind walking home. It was just a couple of streets away and besides, I wasn't a little kid anymore. Mum still gave me a million instructions, though, and kept on telling me over and over to be careful and not to do anything stupid.

Moe was waiting for me on the very first day I walked home. When I turned into our street, there he was sitting in front of our house. And he was there every time after that. Mrs. Nguyen, who lives across the road, told Mum that Moe sat for hours in the afternoon waiting for me. She said he was like a big white sphinx, which I thought was a pretty good way to describe him.

But the best thing about Moe waiting for me was what he did when he saw me coming. First of all his tail would start wagging, and then it would get faster and faster till you'd think it was going to come off. Then he'd start dancing around in a bit of a circle because our house was way down at the end of the street and he wouldn't be sure if it was really me or not. When I got closer and he knew it was me, he'd come charging up the road and jump all over me and whip me with his tail and slobber me half to death.

No one was ever as happy to see me as Mister Mosely was. He always made me feel good. Even if I got into trouble at school or lost something or some kids were being idiots and saying or doing stuff, it didn't make any difference to Moe. He just went nuts every time, like I was some kind of a hero or a movie star or the most important person in the world. And that's sort of how I felt.

Sometimes, just for fun, I'd play this game with Mister Mosely. I'd pretend I was a spy or a special agent or something and our house was a secret enemy hideaway that Moe was guarding. My mission was to see how close I could get to the house before Moe figured out it was really me. What I'd do is, I'd keep my school hat pulled down, and I wouldn't look up at him or smile or call out or anything. I'd just keep walking slowly down the street making out like I was some stranger.

That would get Moe confused straightaway. I'd watch him from under my hat. Pretty soon he'd start to think he'd got it wrong and that maybe it wasn't really me and he'd stop jumping around. Then his tail would stop wagging. The closer I got, the funnier it was. Moe would start sniffing the air, and his tail would wind up again. Then he'd come up the street a little bit, but he'd stop and turn around. Sometimes he'd go round and round in circles and I'd have to try really hard to stop myself from bursting out laughing. Laughing was a BIG mistake. As soon as I laughed, I'd give myself away, and Mister Mosely would charge at me and be so psycho with happiness he'd almost kill me.

The best one I ever did was this time when I pulled my hat really low and I walked down the street, sort of mumbling in the deepest fake voice I could do. That totally fooled old Moe. I got so close I could have almost reached out and patted him. But I didn't. I just stood there. I could see Moe's feet dancing around and I could hear him whining like crazy. He was going totally nuts because he was ninety-nine percent sure it was me but still one percent thinking maybe it wasn't. When I finally took my hat off, he was so happy he knocked me down and gave me the biggest slobbering ever. It was pretty horrible, but it was still worth it.

I stopped playing those kinds of tricks on Mister Mosely because of the day it all went wrong. That's going to be my next story. It's one of the ones I wish wasn't true.

17

MISTER MOSELY AND THE STUPID TRICK

One day when I was coming home from school, I thought of a trick I could do to fool Mister Mosely. I figured it would be really funny. It wasn't. And it was the last trick I ever played on him.

It was the day we got to bring home the masks we'd been making all week in Miss Digby's art class. I couldn't wait to show mine to Mum and Dad. It looked a bit like the Joker from *Batman*, only better and scarier and with a lot more colors on it. I thought it would be pretty funny to fool Mister Mosely with it.

When I got to the top of our street, I hid behind the big fence there and checked around the corner. Mister Mosely was waiting in his usual spot. I put on my mask and I pulled my hat down really low and walked toward our house.

When Moe saw me coming, he started getting excited the same as he always did. I waited till I got about halfway down our street, then I waved and called out to him. As soon as he heard my voice and saw me waving, he came galloping up at me, which is exactly what I knew he would do. That's when I did this really stupid thing.

When Mister Mosely got close, I lifted up my head so he could see the mask, and I stuck out my arms and growled at him all at the same time. I guess it was a bit of a mean thing for me to do, on account of Mister Mosely being so happy to see me and everything. But I was only doing it as a joke and I never thought anything bad would happen. I just thought Moe would get a bit of a fright and it would be funny. But it didn't end up being funny.

When Mister Mosely saw the scary mask and heard me growl, he got a fright all right, a giant one. He tried to stop dead on the spot, but his long legs got all tangled up and he almost crashed over. Then he sort of swerved really fast to run away from me. I started to laugh because he looked so hilarious and because I'd fooled him so bad. But when Moe swerved to get away from me, he ran straight out onto the road.

I was still laughing when the car hit him.

18

MISTER MOSELY AND THE STUPID TRICK — THE END

I didn't want to write any more of that story yesterday. It made me feel bad. But a story doesn't go away or stop being true just because you stop telling it. So this is what happened next.

Mister Mosely ran out onto the road and all of a sudden there was a car and there were tires screeching and the car was thumping into Moe and he was yelping and rolling over and over and over. Then he sort of stopped and stayed still and everything went quiet. I couldn't breathe and all my insides froze up.

What I remember most is the burned-rubber smell from the tires, and the lady in the car just sitting there with her hands over her mouth and her face all white, and Mister Mosely finally getting up and limping down the road into our yard, all sort of crumpled up and broken-looking. I stopped being frozen then. I threw my mask away and ran after him.

Lucky for me, Dad was home early from job hunting. He must have heard the squealing from the tires and everything, because he came running down the driveway just when I was coming up. I tried to tell him about Mister Mosely, but he just wanted to know if I was all right. When I told him I was, he squeezed me so tight I thought I'd bust for sure.

Pretty soon the lady from the car was there too, and she was really upset and saying how sorry she was and that she didn't see Mister Mosely and how he ran right in front of her and there was no way she could stop in time. Dad kept telling her it was all right and that it wasn't her fault, but I could see she still felt pretty bad. Then we all started looking around for Moe, but we couldn't find him anywhere. He wasn't in his bed on the porch and he wasn't under the house and we couldn't see him anywhere around the backyard.

Where we found him was under the garage. He

used to crawl under there on really hot days. Sometimes I went under there looking for lizards or ant lion nests. It was a pretty good place to hide too, but you couldn't go that far under because the ground sloped up. If you went too far, you got all squashed under the floor and you'd bump your head all the time and get spiderwebs stuck in your hair.

It was dark under the garage, but we spotted Moe when Dad saw his eyes shining a bit. We tried to reach him, but he was too far back and he wouldn't come when we called. There was only one way we could get Moe out of there. Dad had to back the car out from the garage and rip up some of the floorboards with his crowbar.

When enough of the floorboards were out, Dad knelt down beside the hole and leaned right in and lifted Mister Mosely out. I didn't think he would be strong enough to do that, but he did, even though his face went really red and sweaty and he swore a bit, but not very loud because the lady from the car was still there.

While Dad was lifting him out, Mister Mosely didn't make any sound at all. He just shook like he was freezing to death. He was still shaking when Dad put him down on the floor of the garage. He looked so bad. His legs were all twitchy and he had big bumps on him and there was all this blood on his side and big patches of hair on his legs and head were rubbed off. When I saw him, I felt like I did the day I found Goblin on the bottom of his tank with all the ants on him, only worse. I just kept saying over and over to myself, "Please don't let him die. Please don't let him die."

Moe didn't die, but the vet said if he wasn't so big and strong, it might have been a lot different. He was still hurt pretty bad. He had three broken ribs and some other bad cuts and bruises, so he had to stay at the vet's for a while. Dad said he had no idea how we were going to pay for it because we had nothing in the bank. But the vet said that Moe was good company and there was no hurry and we could pay her back when Dad was working again. Mum cried and hugged the vet when she said that.

When Mister Mosely was strong enough to come home, he had to wear another bucket thing. That was because he had lots of stitches in his side. They were in a big V shape and all the hair around them was shaved off. And he had blobs of orangey-yellow stuff painted all over his white body to help the other cuts heal up. Mum said the vet had turned poor old Moe into one of those albino tigers. Dad said more like "an albino tiger that had been caught in a blender."

We had to move Mister Mosely's bed downstairs into the laundry room until he got better, because there was no way he could make it all the way to the porch. Mum said Moe was a good patient because he just rested and waited and didn't try to do too much before he was ready for it. "Unlike your father" was what Mum said. When he did get better, we put Moe's bed back on the porch, and after a while he started fetching the paper and waiting for me in front of the house same as always.

The only other thing I remember about the day Mister Mosely got hit was how the lady in the car gave my mask back to me. She must have found it on the gutter. I waited till she left and then I ripped it up into little pieces and threw it in the rubbish bin.

19

MISTER MOSELY AND MUM

Mum used to say that Mister Mosely had a sixth sense about things. That meant he knew stuff when no one else did.

Dad didn't think so. He said he was pretty sure Moe didn't have a sixth sense about newspapers anyway. But I think Mum was right, because one time Mister Mosely knew something about her before anyone else.

It all began about a year ago. It was the last day of school before the holidays. I was walking home. My bag was really heavy because it was packed up with all the junk from my locker. I didn't care, though. I was too busy thinking about all the things I was going to do and how me and Moe would muck around together. But when I got to the top of the street and looked down at our house, Moe wasn't there waiting for me. I was scared straightaway. I thought maybe he got hit by a car again, so I ran home as fast as I could.

I found Moe in the backyard under the clothes-line. He was just watching Mum peg out the washing. When he saw me, he came over and jumped around a bit, but then he went straight back to Mum. It wasn't like Moe at all. Mum didn't know what was wrong with him either. She said he'd been under her feet all day, "hanging around like a bad smell." I don't think she really minded too much, because she was smiling when she said it.

Moe kept hanging around Mum pretty much all the time after that. It was like he was her bodyguard or something. He'd sit at the back door waiting for her to come outside and then he'd follow her around everywhere she went. Even if me and Moe were playing together in the yard or if we went down to the park, you could tell all he really wanted to do was to get back to Mum. Mum said it was even worse when she was home by herself, because then Moe stuck to her like glue.

None of us knew then that Mum was going to have a baby. Mum only found out for sure later. But I reckon Mister Mosely knew all along, and that was why he was acting so weird. Mum thought so too. She said Moe must have known about Grace coming just like some other animals knew about storms or earthquakes before they happened.

I think it was pretty cool how Mister Mosely knew about Grace before anyone else. And there was other stuff he knew about too. He could always tell when something was wrong. Like one time when he woke me up in the middle of the night with his whining.

I went outside to the porch to see what was worrying him, but I couldn't work out what was wrong. Then I heard some voices. They were coming from Mum and Dad's room. That's what Moe was whining about. He knew something wasn't right, even if he didn't know what any of the words meant.

I couldn't understand many of the words either, just the loud ones. Like Dad saying, "How could it happen?" He didn't sound happy when he said that. I thought he might be talking about Mum having a baby, except he knew how that stuff happened because he was there when Mum told me all about it.

I listened some more. Dad kept going on and on about having no job and no money and not being able to afford stuff. Then it went quieter. I could still hear voices, but they were all blurry. They sounded angry, though. And sometimes sad. The last thing I heard was Dad swearing, which he doesn't normally do. Then Mum and him stopped talking. I waited, but I didn't hear anything else. It was all just quiet and still and dark.

I didn't go back to bed right away. I stayed out there on the porch with Mister Mosely. He had his big head on my lap and I wrapped my arms around him to stay warm. It made me think of when I was little and there was a storm and we'd be hiding under the bed together.

Moe was always good to hold on to when things started to get a bit scary and you didn't know what might happen next.

20

MISTER MOSELY AND GRACE

Grace ended up being born four weeks before she was supposed to be. No one knew that was going to happen. No one except Mister Mosely.

Moe had been acting funny all that day. Mum said he wasn't lying down on the porch, which is what he normally did. He was standing up all the time and looking in through the screen door and walking around "like he was on hot coals." She said every time Mister Mosely saw her he'd start whining for no reason.

When Mum was making tea that night, she started to feel funny and she knew right away something was happening with the baby. Dad wasn't home then. He had a new job helping build a dam somewhere. Uncle Gavin got that job for him. It was a long way away so Dad only got to come home on weekends. Anyway, because Dad wasn't there, Mum had to ring up Uncle Gavin to take her to the hospital. Amelia and me stayed with Mrs. Nguyen from across the road.

Grace was born that night. Mum said it was lucky she wasn't born in Uncle Gavin's car. The funny thing was, most of the people at the hospital thought that Uncle Gavin was Grace's father because Dad didn't get there until after it was all over. Uncle Gavin made lots of jokes about that, but I don't think Dad thought they were so funny, because he didn't laugh much.

Dad had stopped laughing at a lot of things since he lost his old job. I was hoping that Grace being born would make him happy again. Way back when he found out Mum was having me, he was so happy he picked her up and carried her all the way out to the front yard to tell the neighbors the good news. Mum's told me that story plenty of times. And if you look at the photos of when Amelia was born, Dad's smiling and laughing in every one. But when

Grace was born, Dad didn't do any of that stuff. He just looked tired and worried.

We couldn't bring Grace home straightaway. She was so tiny and red when she was born, she had to stay in the hospital in a special plastic crib with all these tubes in her till she got bigger and stronger. Seeing how Grace was so little and Mister Mosely was so big, Nanny and Pop were worried about him being around her. They thought Moe might hurt her somehow, even if he didn't really mean to.

Mum wasn't worried, though. She kept saying Mister Mosely would be fine and we just had to "introduce" Grace to him properly so that he knew she was part of our family. And that's what we did. On the first day they came home, Mum sat in a chair with Grace, and then Dad and Amelia and me brought Moe in to meet her. Moe never looked bigger. Just his head was about two of Grace.

Mum spoke really softly. She said, "Mister Mosely, this is Grace. She's the newest member of the Ingram family. Grace, this is Mister Mosely. He's a special part of our family too and he's been waiting to meet you for *such* a long time."

You could tell Moe was superexcited because his body was all sort of twitchy. But when he saw Grace he didn't whine or bark and give her a big fright, which is what I was afraid he would do. And he didn't jump all over the place and whip his tail around either. He just stood there like a big statue, looking at her and sniffing a bit without hardly making a sound. Then he just sat down and rested his head on Mum's knee and the only thing that moved were his eyes. Mum said there was nothing to worry about because Moe was as gentle as a lamb and he wouldn't hurt a fly.

That was true. Except there was this one time when I thought Mister Mosely was going to hurt a lot more than just a fly.

21

THE DAY MISTER MOSELY CHANGED

The day I thought Mister Mosely was going to hurt something more than just a fly was the only time he ever scared me. And I don't think it was just me who was scared.

It started out like just a normal sort of a day. I was mucking around with Moe in the backyard. I was throwing a tennis ball way up in the air and he was trying to catch it before it bounced. Amelia was at Nanny and Pop's. While I was playing with Moe, Dad's car came down the driveway. That was strange because Dad had his new job then at the dam and he wasn't supposed to get home till the weekend.

When he got out of the car, Dad looked angry.

I figured that was because Uncle Gavin's car was blocking the driveway and Dad couldn't get into the garage. Uncle Gavin came to our house a fair bit when Dad was away. He was always dropping in to see if Mum was okay or if we needed anything. Sometimes he gave us some money because he said he knew we were "doing it tough." We weren't supposed to tell Dad about that for some reason.

This time, Uncle Gavin brought a big box filled with "special treats" just for Mum. There was a proper coffeemaker and some wine and stuff like soap and perfume. The best thing was a huge box of chocolates, but Mum said we couldn't open them till later.

I guess it was pretty annoying for Dad not being able to get into the garage, but you couldn't really blame Uncle Gavin for parking in the driveway. He didn't know Dad would be home before Saturday morning either, so he didn't think he'd be blocking anything. But Dad wasn't looking too happy when he had to drive onto the grass just so Uncle Gavin would be able to get his car out.

When I went over and asked Dad how come he was home early, he just shook his head and said something about a "bloody strike." He didn't even look at me when he said it. He just kept looking up at our house. Then he headed for the back stairs. I was going to go with him, but he said, "Stay there." I didn't know why he said that, but he sounded like he really meant it, so I did and I went back to throwing the tennis ball for Mister Mosely.

Moe and me were playing out back near the mango tree. We had to do that because Mum had clean sheets on the clothesline and we were supposed to stay away from them. That was because once me and my cousins were playing cricket with a tennis ball and I guess it must have hit Mum's sheets a few times and put dirty marks on them. After that Mum said, "No ball games near the sheets." Now she says that every time she does the washing, even when I'm not thinking about playing with a ball.

Anyway, what happened next was, while I was playing with Mister Mosely, all this noise and yelling started coming from inside our house. Then the back door banged open. Uncle Gavin came out first, then Dad. He was looking really mad now. Mum came out last. She looked frightened. I didn't know what was going on. Mum was calling out Dad's name over and over and saying, "Stop it!" and "It's nothing!" and Uncle Gavin was shaking his head and holding his hands in the air and telling Dad he was being bloody stupid, which just seemed to make Dad even madder.

Then they all came down into the backyard. Mister Mosely tried to run over to them, but I didn't think it was a good idea, so I held on to his collar and told him to stay. Dad pushed Uncle Gavin in the back and told him to clear out. He told Uncle Gavin that we weren't a "bloody charity." He said he could take care of his own family. Dad was still shouting stuff when Uncle Gavin told him to stop acting like an idiot. I think it was that last bit that Dad didn't like too much, because that was when he grabbed Uncle Gavin by the shoulder and he spun him around and punched him really hard right in the face. I had to hold on extra tight to Mister Mosely then.

I'd never seen someone get punched for real before. It wasn't the same as on TV or in the movies. It didn't even sound the same. It sounded sort of squishier and like it would really hurt. I think it did too, because it made Uncle Gavin's head go right back and he grabbed his face and said the same swearword about ten times. Then big blobs of blood started dripping between Uncle Gavin's fingers. When he took his hands away, his nose and his mouth were all red and I think one of his teeth was missing. Uncle Gavin spat on the ground and sort of flicked his hands to get rid of the blood, and a big spray of red went right across one of Mum's clean sheets.

Mum had her hands over her mouth. She looked like the lady in the car did after she ran into Mister Mosely. Then she pushed in front of Dad and tried to help Uncle Gavin, but Uncle Gavin held up his hands to stop her. They were all bloody and his nose was big and twisted all wrong. Uncle Gavin wiped his face on his T-shirt and put a big smudge of blood on that too. Then he got into his car without saying anything or looking at anyone. He had one hand over his face as he backed out. There was still tons of blood dripping everywhere.

Mum started to cry then, and Mister Mosely made one of his howly whining noises and pulled away from me. I tried to stop him but he was too strong. He ran over to Mum and stood beside her, wagging his tail the way he did when he wasn't sure if it was me coming down the street or not. I wanted to be over there with him, but Mum and Dad started yelling stuff at each other and I was scared. Mum said, "He was only trying to help." Dad didn't say anything. He just started to walk away. Then Mum said, "Why are you acting like such a child?"

I didn't like the look on Dad's face then. He turned around and started heading straight at Mum. That's when Mister Mosely jumped in front of him. Then Moe changed. It was like he was a Transformer or something. All the hair on his back stuck up and it made him look even bigger than normal, and the skin around his mouth stretched back till all you could see were long, pointy teeth. Then he made this really loud growling sort of noise that I'd never heard him do before. For a couple of seconds he wasn't Mister Mosely anymore. He was something scary and dangerous.

What Moe did made everyone just stop and stare at him. Then he sort of went back to his normal self and just started wagging his tail at Dad and licking Mum's hand. Nobody was saying anything. Then I heard Grace crying upstairs in her crib. Dad heard her too. He looked up at Grace's room and then at Mum and he said, "Maybe you'd all be better off if he really was the father." Mum opened her mouth, but no words came out. It looked like someone had punched her really hard in the stomach and she couldn't breathe.

Dad got into the car and left then. You could tell he was still mad, because he put big skid marks on the grass when he backed out. When Dad was gone, Mum started looking around everywhere like she didn't know where she was. Then she saw the sheet with Uncle Gavin's blood all over it and she started ripping it down from the clothesline. She didn't even take the pegs off first. She just pulled at it until they popped off. Then she sat down on the grass with the sheet all wrapped around her and started crying and rocking and hugging it like it was a baby or something.

I'd never seen Mum cry so hard before. It made me feel sick. I went over and stood beside her. I didn't know what to do. But Mister Mosely did. He pushed in next to Mum and licked her face. Her nose was dripping and she wiped it right on the sheets. Then she grabbed Mister Mosely and she grabbed me and she pulled us in tight and hugged us both. I hugged her back. Moe couldn't hug any-one, so he just licked our faces some more and thumped us both with his big tail.

Mum kept telling me how she was sorry I had to see all that, and that it was just a big misunder-standing, and Dad and her were under a lot of stress. She told me not to worry about it and that some-times mums and dads fight and say things they shouldn't, but everything was going to be fine and nothing was going to change.

But that wasn't really true. Some things did change. Like how Uncle Gavin stopped coming to our house and we stopped going to his place and how Dad stopped making those jokes about his "little brother." And even Mum and Dad changed. They went sort of quiet. I know that sounds better than yelling. But sometimes it's not.

One thing that didn't change was Mister Mosely. Even after he did that scary Transformer thing, he was still exactly the same old Moe.

22

MISTER MOSELY AND DAD

Mum always said Mister Mosely was a "good listener." He was. Amelia used to talk to him nonstop when she was dressing him up. I talked to him too. All the time. I still do. But I never thought Dad talked to Moe that much. I was wrong.

I found that out one night when I was bringing Dad's dinner down to him. It was after Dad quit his job at the dam and got another one working for the council, making roads. He's still got that job. Now he comes home every night instead of just the weekends, but he's always tired and dirty and covered in black road gunk. He gets home late too. That's because he does heaps of overtime on account of Grace being "an extra mouth to feed." I guess that's why he started having dinner downstairs in the workshop all by himself.

What happens most times is that Mum wraps Dad's dinner in foil and leaves it on the stove while we eat ours. Then she takes it down later when Dad's had a chance to "unwind a bit." Mostly, Mum takes Dad's dinner down to him, especially when Dad has overtime. But sometimes if it isn't too late, Mum asks me to do it.

That's how I found out about Dad talking to Mister Mosely. One night I was going down the back steps with his dinner and I heard him. I thought he was on his phone, but when I looked in through the lattice, he was just sitting at our old kitchen table, the one we used to have upstairs before we got the new one. I watched him open another bottle of beer and fill up his glass. Then he started talking again.

I got a bit worried when I saw that because I thought Dad must have been talking to himself. But then he patted his leg and Mister Mosely's big head came up from under the table, so I knew that was who he was talking to all along. It was weird listening to Dad talk to Mister Mosely just like he was another person, and asking him all these questions and everything. It was weird because after that Uncle Gavin thing, Dad didn't talk much about anything to anyone.

I suppose it was wrong to listen to Dad when he didn't know I was there, but I wanted to find out what he was talking to Mister Mosely about. I worked out it was about that time Moe went missing for two weeks, because Dad kept asking Moe what he got up to and where he went and what his secret was. At the end he said, "But you came back, didn't you, big guy?" I remember that because when Dad said it, he drank all his beer down in one big go. Then he said, "You and me both."

Dad sort of rubbed his eyes when he said that, and it looked a bit like he was crying. He wasn't, though, because Dad never cries. Except for that time when Amelia drew all that stuff on Mister Mosely and that was only because he was laughing so much, so it wasn't even proper crying. Dad was probably just rubbing his eyes because he was tired or he had some dirt in them, seeing how he was still all filthy and greasy from building roads.

Every time I took Dad's dinner down, Mister Mosely was there with him. There were other times I heard Dad talking, but I didn't try to listen in anymore. I felt bad about spying on him. Some people might think that was a strange thing for my dad to do, talk to a dog. But I don't think so. Like I said before, we all talked to Mister Mosely.

I bet old Moe thought it was crazy, though, all these people talking to him when he couldn't talk back. He probably wondered why we didn't just talk to each other. I don't know about Mum and Dad and Amelia, but I liked talking to Moe because I could say stuff to him I couldn't really say to anyone else. And I knew Moe would always be there to listen to me.

Well, that's what I thought.

23

MISTER MOSELY
AND THE STAIRS

One day, there was this big thump on the back stairs and I went out to see what it was. The thump was Mister Mosely falling over. He was about halfway up. He had our newspaper in his mouth and he was looking at me with his eyes all big and scared.

I just thought Moe must have run up the stairs too fast and slipped. I thought he was just being "Un-co Moe" again. Anyway, he got himself up all right, but he was pretty shaky and he was limping too. I couldn't see any cuts or bumps on him, but I told Mum and Dad about him falling down. They checked him over and said he seemed fine. Dad thought he was probably just a bit stiff and sore, that's all.

But Moe's limp didn't go away. Then it got worse. When he got the paper, he was slower than normal and you could tell it was hurting him. In the end, Mum made Dad take Moe to the vet to see what was wrong.

That's how we found out about the cancer.

We didn't find out straightaway because the vet had to do some tests first. But when the tests came back that's what the vet said Mister Mosely had. She said it was in his bones. She said she was sorry.

I never even knew that dogs got cancer. I knew that people did, because that's what happened to our Benpa, who was Dad's dad. But the vet said dogs could get cancer too, same as people, and she said big dogs like Mister Mosely were the ones that got it the most. She didn't know why that was.

When we found out about the cancer, I asked Mum and Dad if Mister Mosely was going to go to the hospital like Benpa did, to try and help him get better. But Dad said that would cost a lot of money and we couldn't afford it and anyway it wouldn't help much. He said the best thing to do was try and make sure that Mister Mosely was happy and not in any pain.

I didn't like the way Dad was saying that. I didn't want Mister Mosely to be sick. He didn't even look sick. He looked exactly the same as he always did except for the limp. I wanted Mum and Dad to take all the money I was saving up for computer games so we could help Mister Mosely. Dad just shook his head when I said that and Mum just cried.

At the vet's, we got some special medicine to take home with us. We had to give it to Moe with his food. That was my job. I made sure he took it every single day and never ever missed out once. I wanted the medicine to make him better. I wanted it to make the cancer go away. But that didn't happen.

What happened was, it started to get harder and harder for Mister Mosely to fetch the paper. We tried to make him stop but he wouldn't. We'd find him stuck halfway up the back stairs every day, breathing really fast and whining and with that black spot under his eye making him look really sad. One time he made it all the way up but then he was stuck there. We had to wait till Dad got home from work because Moe was too big for Mum and me to carry back down again.

So what I did was, I taught Moe just to bring the paper to the bottom of the steps and drop it there instead of trying to bring it all the way up to the top like he used to. And Dad made a new place for him down in the laundry room.

It didn't seem right not having Moe on the porch waiting for us. I thought I'd never see him there again. But I did. Just one more time.

24

MISTER MOSELY BACK
ON THE PORCH

I kept giving Mister Mosely his medicine exactly like
the vet said. But it wasn't working.

I knew it, because after a while just going out to
the front yard and carrying the paper back to the
bottom of the stairs was too much for him. Some
days, like when the paper came early on Saturday
morning and it was cold, Moe couldn't even stand
up. He'd keep trying, though, and he'd be whining
and whimpering all the time and he'd only stop
when someone went and got the paper and showed
it to him. I guess then he knew his job was done.

One Saturday when I was in the kitchen making
myself some toast, I heard Mister Mosely whining,
so I went out to see what was wrong. He was at the

bottom of the stairs. The big Saturday newspaper was on the step in front of him. It was the first time for ages that Moe had tried to bring the paper around.

I helped him back to his bed and took the paper up for Dad. He was making a cup of tea. I was just giving Dad the paper when we heard Mister Mosely whining again. This time we found him up a few steps and trying to climb higher. He was all shaky and almost falling over. Dad had to take him back down before he hurt himself.

But Moe just wouldn't stay there. As soon as we got back to the kitchen, we heard the whining again and then we heard a big thud and some scratching too. Dad and I ran out the back. Moe had fallen over and his legs were going everywhere and he was trying to stop himself from sliding down the stairs. Dad grabbed him, and Mum came running out because of all the noise.

Dad said, "Don't know what's got into him, but he wants to get up to that porch. Haven't got a clue how he expects to get back down." Mum just looked kind of sad and said that maybe he wasn't worried about that anymore. I wasn't sure what she meant.

Anyway, we didn't want Mister Mosely to keep hurting himself trying to get upstairs, so Mum made a bed for him on the porch just like she did way back when he was a puppy. When it was made, Dad carried Moe all the way up. I got his bowls for him — his water bowl and the big silver one that Dad wrote his name on. We gave him some dry dog food and leftover gravy, but he didn't eat any of it.

Mister Mosely stayed there in his old spot all afternoon. When it got dark, Dad carried him down-stairs so he could go to the toilet if he wanted to and to see if maybe he would go back to the laundry room. He wouldn't. Every time Dad started to go upstairs, Mister Mosely tried to follow him. That made Dad a bit cross and he called Moe a stubborn old coot, but he carried him all the way back up to the porch just the same.

That night, Mum let me sit outside with Mister Mosely way past the time I usually went to bed. Moe didn't look as big and strong as he used to. I guess I was getting bigger too. It was funny thinking how

I could ride on his back when I was little and how he would drag me along on my cardboard sled. But he was still the same old Moe. I put my finger on the black tear spot under his eye and I traced around the wonky heart shape on his chest, the one that Mum said was there because Moe's heart was too big to all fit on the inside.

I stayed up so late I fell asleep on Mister Mosely, and Mum had to wake me up to go to bed. I remember how I patted Moe and gave him a bit of a hug and how his big tail thumped a couple of times on the floor. I left him there waiting on the porch just like always.

Only I found out it wasn't any of us that Mister Mosely was waiting for this time.

25

MISTER MOSELY — JUST A DOG

When I woke up the next day, the first thing I did was check on Mister Mosely. But the porch was empty. Then I saw Mum and Dad down in the backyard. Mum had on her dressing gown. Dad was beside her. Something was wrapped in a sheet on the ground between them.

As soon as I got downstairs, Mum came over and hugged me. She told me Mister Mosely had died during the night, only she said he'd "passed away." She said she knew it was sad, but the good thing was, Moe wasn't in pain anymore. She said it was for the best. I didn't believe her. I wanted to see Mister Mosely for myself, so Dad pulled back the sheet a bit. It looked like Moe was just asleep. But when I patted him, he felt cold and he didn't move.

I didn't want to cry; I really didn't, but my eyes started stinging and something was sticking in my throat. I tried to think about those things Mum said. About how Mister Mosely wasn't hurting anymore, and how it was sad but it was for the best. But I kept hoping none of it was true. I kept hoping that Mister Mosely was just trying to fool me like how I tried to fool him all those times when I came home from school and he was waiting for me. I wanted him to lift up his head and open his big eyes and start thumping his tail on the grass a million miles an hour the way he always did.

Then Mum knelt down beside me and her face came right up close to mine. I could see her eyes were wet and she kept telling me how it was "all right" and how Mister Mosely had a good life and how it was okay to feel sad, and I kept nodding and nodding and nodding because I knew it was all true, but mainly because I wanted her to stop saying those kinds of things so I could think about something else and about not crying.

But I couldn't breathe and I couldn't swallow and when I tried to, it sounded like I was choking, and then I was making those noises little kids do when they cry, and I tried even harder to stop but it just made it worse. Then Dad said, "All right, come on, that's enough. It's not the end of the world," and he was right too, but Mum looked all angry at him and told him to leave me alone and that I could cry if I wanted to cry and Dad said I wasn't a baby anymore, which I wasn't either. I really wasn't.

I didn't want Mum and Dad to fight. I didn't want them to get angry with each other the way they did that time with Uncle Gavin when Mister Mosely changed into something scary. So I tried to tell them that I was all right, that I wasn't a baby, that I knew Moe had to die. But I couldn't breathe properly and I couldn't make any words come out, only stupid choking hiccup noises that just got louder and louder until Mum hugged me even tighter and that made it twice as bad and I couldn't stop myself. Then Dad lost his temper and said, "That's enough! It's not like one of us has died. It's just a dog, for God's sake."

And that's when it happened, exactly how I told you about already. That's when my mum punched my dad. She just sort of stood up and turned around and she was shaking her head and staring at Dad like she didn't know who he was. Then she hit him on the chest with the back of her fist and said, "Don't you say that!" And Dad just stared at her like he didn't know who she was either, and Mum started crying and hitting Dad's chest as if she was trying to beat down a wall or something and saying, "Don't you *say* that! Don't you *dare* say *that*!"

I just wanted it all to stop. I wanted Mum and Dad to stop looking at each other that way. I wanted Mister Mosely to jump up and stand between them and growl at them and show them his teeth and be big and strong and scary and make it all end. But he didn't. He didn't do anything. He just lay there wrapped up in that sheet.

So I did it. I squeezed between Mum and Dad, but I couldn't growl like Mister Moe or be scary like him, so I yelled as loud as I could for them to stop and I shouted, "I hate you!" even though that wasn't really true. But it worked just the same because

Mum stopped hitting Dad and they stopped looking at each other and they looked at me instead. Then Mum started to cry like she did that day with the sheet and she just sort of let herself fall forward and her head hit on Dad's chest.

We stayed like that for a while, Dad just standing there and Mum crying and me stuck between them. And all the time Mister Mosely just lay on the grass all wrapped up and he didn't move and he didn't whine and he didn't wag his tail because it really was true and I knew it.

Mister Mosely was gone.

26

MISTER MOSELY'S
NEW PLACE

We buried Moe in the back corner of our yard behind the trellis near the mango tree. Dad dug the hole while I watched and got water for him. It was a hot day and he was sweating a lot.

The hole Dad dug was a big one and the sides were all neat and straight and everything. It looked like a person hole, not like a "just a dog" sort of a one. When it was finished, I went and called Mum. Grace was asleep in her crib. Amelia wasn't there at all. She was at Grandma's for the day. Mum said Amelia was "a bit young for all this."

Dad pulled back the sheet a little so we could see Mister Mosely one last time. I didn't want to pat him and feel him all cold again, but Mum put her finger on his black tear dot just like I did on the porch. Then she touched the big heart spots on his chest and said, "Way too big to fit inside. Way too big," and sort of whispered, "It's all over, Moe. No more pain now," before she got all teary and sniffy and put her arm around me.

Then Dad wrapped the sheet back around Mister Mosely and carried him over to the hole. He had to kneel down and lean right over to lay Mister Mosely in it. It looked a bit like Mum putting Grace into her crib. And it made me think of all these other things too, like when Dad lifted Mister Mosely up from under the garage and that time at the vet's when he carried Moe and me to the car, and all the other times he carried Moe up and down the back stairs when the cancer made his legs too weak. I had to stop thinking about stuff like that because my eyes started burning.

We didn't say any prayers or make any speeches or anything when we buried Mister Mosely. Mum just said, "So long, Mister Moe. Thanks for everything." And I thought I was going to bawl like a little kid again, so I had to blink my eyes and just stare really hard into the hole. That's when I saw the stains on the sheet Mister Mosely was wrapped in and I knew it was the same one that Uncle Gavin's blood went all over.

Then Dad had to shovel all the dirt back into the hole. Mum said I didn't have to stay and watch that if I didn't want to. I wasn't sure if I wanted to or not. But I did anyway. So did Mum. We stayed and watched and bit by bit Mister Mosely and that old sheet with Uncle Gavin's blood on it disappeared under the dirt.

27

MISTER MOSELY'S BOWL

After Dad finished his shoveling, Mum went and got a packet of seeds and spread them all over where Mister Mosely was buried.

The packet had MIXED FLOWERS written on the front. Mum told me that when the flowers started to grow, it would be like a sign or a message from Moe telling us that he was okay and that we shouldn't be sad for him anymore. I guess Mum must have thought I was still a little kid like Amelia to believe that. I didn't mind, though. She was only saying it to try and make me feel better.

Mum went back upstairs then to make sure Grace was all right and I stayed with Dad to help him clean up and put everything away. After we did that, I went back out to where Moe was buried. Dad came out too. I liked it there under the mango tree. It was quiet and cool and it was sort of hidden away between the trellis and the back fence. It was a good place for Mister Mosely.

While we were just standing there, Dad started talking. He said, "These things happen. It's tough, but you just have to deal with them." He meant Mister Mosely dying. I told him I knew that, and he just nodded and said, "Good man." Then he was quiet some more. Then he said maybe we should have something with Moe's name on it to mark where he was buried. I thought that was a good idea because then it would be a proper grave, so I said maybe we could use Moe's old silver bowl, seeing how it had his name on it already. Dad liked my idea and so that's what we did.

I went and got Moe's bowl from up on the porch and I cleaned it up and Dad had a look around his workshop and found a big cement stone that was left over from when he made the front path. We painted it white. When it dried a bit, we got some Liquid Nails and we glued Mister Mosely's bowl right in the center of the stone so that his name faced the front. Then Dad showed me how to mix up some water and instant cement in a bucket, and we took everything out behind the trellis.

First, Dad dug out a square shape in the dirt at the top of Mister Mosely's grave. When he was finished, I poured in some of the cement and Dad put the paving stone on top of it and tapped it down with a rubber hammer until it was level. Then he made the cement neat around the sides and we pushed the dirt back up to the edges.

After it was all done, Dad asked me if I thought it was like a proper grave now, and I told him yes because it was. When we showed Mum what we'd done, her eyes went all shiny and she just said, "I knew there was a reason I loved you guys."

That night Dad got a phone call from Uncle Gavin. Grandma must have told him about Mister Mosely. Uncle Gavin rang up to say he was sorry.

28

TOASTING MISTER MOSELY

Everything was different without Mister Mosely around. Sort of slow and empty.

When I came home from school the next day there was nothing to do, so I just sat on the back steps and bounced a tennis ball against the wall. I was doing that when I heard the paper man's car down the road. A bit later, I heard the paper landing in our front yard so I went and got it. That made me think about Moe and I just started crying. I couldn't help it.

I didn't want Mum to see me doing that because I knew it would make her sad. So I took the paper up the back where Mister Mosely was buried and I sat on the big rock under the mango tree. I told Moe

I'd gotten the paper for him, which I guess was a pretty stupid thing to do.

That's where I was when Dad's car came down the driveway. He was home early, which meant he mustn't have done any overtime that day. I watched him get out of the car. He was carrying his little cooler and his thermos and some work gear. He had dirt and black stuff all over him as usual. He didn't see me because I was behind the trellis.

Dad went under the house and put some of his stuff away in his workroom and washed up a bit. Then he got a bottle of beer and a glass out of the fridge and he sat down by himself at the old kitchen table. Dad just sat there drinking and sort of staring at nothing. He looked kind of lonely.

Mum was upstairs in the kitchen. I could see her through the little window near the stove. She was making tea. She was speaking to someone because her mouth was moving. It must have been Amelia, but I couldn't see her. It was funny watching Mum and Dad like that. One upstairs and one downstairs.

Then I remembered that I had the paper. I knew

Dad liked to read it when he was drinking his beer so I took it over to him. When I got there, he asked me if I was okay and I said that I was. I was going to go upstairs then, but Dad said to "pull up a pew," which means to sit down, so I did. Then he took out another glass and put a little bit of beer in it and he gave it to me. He said we should toast Mister Mosely, which sounds pretty creepy when you think about it.

Anyway, what Dad did is, he clicked his glass against my glass and said, "To Mister Mosely." Then I had to drink some beer. I didn't like it very much but I pretended I did because it was good being there and doing that stuff with Dad. He called it having an "awake" or something. We didn't say much for a while but then Dad said, "He was a good dog, the old Moe." Then he smiled, but not much, and said, "When he wasn't pretending to be a fish and getting himself caught on hooks." That made me smile a bit too, because I hadn't heard Dad say something like that for a long time.

Then the weirdest thing happened. Dad and me started to remember stuff about that day with Moe and the fishhook and we started to tell each other.

Like I told him how I shouldn't have kept calling Moe and making him try to come home when he couldn't, and Dad told me that it wasn't my fault because I didn't know about the hook being in Moe's mouth in the first place.

We were still talking about the fishhook thing when Mum called from the back porch that tea was ready and for me to come up. I said, "In a minute," because I didn't want to stop talking to Dad. But I guess it must have ended up being longer than a minute, because pretty soon Mum was coming down the steps to find out what I was doing.

I was sure Mum was going to go cross at Dad for giving me some beer. I didn't want her and Dad fighting again. I started to get worried when she came over to the table and she looked at my glass and then at Dad and me. But all she said was, "What's this, then — secret men's business?" I didn't know if she was talking to me or Dad, but Dad was just looking at the table so I told her how we were having an awake for Mister Mosely. Mum smiled a bit when I told her that, which made me feel better and she said, "I see."

Mum just went back upstairs then, and Dad and me sat there without saying anything. Dad drank all his beer down and told me I'd better head off before my tea got cold, otherwise we'd both be in trouble from Mum. And that's what I was going to do, but we heard someone coming down the stairs. It was Amelia. Then we saw Mum coming down behind her. She was carrying a big tray.

Amelia ran over and pulled around a chair so she could sit right beside me, and Mum came over and put the tray on the table. It had three plates of spaghetti bolognese and a bowl of ice cream on it. Mum told us that Amelia had already eaten and Grace was asleep. She said, "If you're having an awake for Mister Mosely, then it should be a family thing."

I told Mum she had to have a drink too so she could toast Moe. I didn't think she even heard me, because she just kept looking at Dad. But I guess she must have, because she said, "I could sure do with one." She sounded pretty sad and worn-out when she said that. So Dad got some more beer from the fridge and some soft drinks too, and Mum went back upstairs and brought Grace down in her carry basket.

That night was one of the strangest nights ever because we all had dinner together under the house. The only one missing was Mister Mosely. But after a while, he sort of wasn't because we started to tell all these stories about him. It happened when I asked Mum if she remembered the time that Moe got the fishhook caught in his mouth because that's what Dad and me were talking about. Mum said, "The poor thing. How could I forget?" And then she started saying some stuff about it and then Amelia wanted to know more because she was only little when it happened.

Dad didn't say much at the beginning, he just listened mostly. But when I told Amelia about me fainting at the vet's and hitting my head and how Mister Mosely had to wear that bucket thing and how Dad had to carry both of us to the car, he said, "Two peas in a pod," which made Mum smile.

Then we just started to tell all the Mister Mosely stories we could think of. One after the other. Like how we got Moe from Uncle Gavin and how Moe got his name and how he cried on the first night when we put him downstairs. And we talked all about the teddy bear and the clock and Amelia drawing on him and that time at the park and the Pink Panther and how he learned to fetch the paper and the time he disappeared and the time he got hit by the car and lots of other things as well.

Mum and me did most of the talking, I guess. Amelia just asked a million questions, as usual. Dad listened mainly and drank his beer, but every now and then he'd add some stuff. Like when I said it was a pretty good trick how Moe learned to fetch the paper, he said, "Yeah, until he tried to steal every one in the neighborhood." That was a bit of an exaggeration, but it made us laugh just the same.

So like I said, even if Mister Mosely wasn't there, he kind of was because he was still there in the stories. And that's how come Mum ended up getting me this journal. She brought it home one day and said I should write down all the Mister Mosely stories we talked about and then we'd have them forever. So that's what I started to do. And that's what I've been doing just about every day since Moe died.

Except now I guess I'm finished, because I've got no more Mister Mosely stories left to tell.

29

NOT REALLY A
MISTER MOSELY STORY

This is not really a Mister Mosely story. It's just some things that happened after he was gone.

One day Mum got some black paint and she added a dot and a wonky heart to that white paving stone Dad and me put on Mister Mosely's grave, the one we glued his silver bowl on. I thought it was great what Mum did. Dad thought so too.

And you know all those seeds Mum planted on top of where Moe was buried? Well, they all grew into flowers. When they were tiny, I didn't know if they were flowers or weeds. I had to wait a long time to find out. But now there are flowers every-where. Mum says they're just perfect for Moe, seeing how they're all the colors of the rainbow. I didn't really get what she meant, but she told me when you mix all those different colors together, you end up with white, just like Moe. I don't think that's Mister Mosely sending us a sign or a message or anything, but it's still kind of cool when you think about it.

I wish I had more Mister Mosely stories to tell. It was good coming out here every day with my journal and sitting under the mango tree and writing them all down. Even the hard ones. And every time I saw Moe's bowl with his name on it, it kind of felt like he was still waiting for me, same as always. Dumb, I know.

I still miss him heaps. Sometimes I think I hear his whine or his weird howling bark, but it's always some other dog somewhere. And sometimes I think I'm going to see him on the porch or running around the backyard or waiting out the front. But I never do. There's just this big empty space where he used to be.

Amelia wants to get a new dog. She's always bugging Mum and Dad about it. I think it would be weird having a dog that wasn't Mister Mosely. Amelia wants a little fluffy one that could fit inside a handbag, but Mum keeps saying that a dog is a "big commitment" and we'll just have to "wait and see" what happens with Dad's work.

Dad could be getting his old job back selling TVs and stuff now that the recession thing might be going away. I really hope he does. Maybe that would make him happy and he'd tell jokes and funny stories all the time like before, and maybe him and Mum wouldn't be so quiet together and they might even laugh again the way they did that time when Amelia drew all that stuff on Mister Mosely. That's what I want more than anything in the entire world.

But I wanted Mister Mosely to get better too. And he didn't. So just because you really want something to happen doesn't mean that it will. I guess it's like Mum keeps telling Amelia. Sometimes you just have to wait and see.

Mister Mosely was really good at doing that. He waited for heaps of stuff. He waited on the porch for us to come outside. He waited for ages to get better after the car hit him. He waited all those times for Uncle Gavin to stop teasing him and for Amelia to get tired of dressing him up and for Dad to finish his tea and for Grace to be born. And he waited for me too. Every single day after school.

So that's what I'm going to do with Mum and Dad. Just wait. Wait and hope. Same as I did when I waited to find out if those little green shoots on Moe's grave would turn into weeds or flowers.

Maybe I learned how to do that from Mister Mosely. Maybe it's the one trick he taught me. That sometimes, no matter how much you want something, the very best thing you can do is wait, just like he did. Wait for stuff to happen or stop happening, for things to heal up and get better or for someone to come home.

I reckon that's a pretty good trick to learn, from just a dog.

ABOUT THE AUTHOR

MICHAEL GERARD BAUER'S first book was *The Running Man* and was named the 2005 Children's Book Council of Australia Book of the Year for Older Readers. Michael lives in Brisbane, Australia. He grew up with two dogs, Penny and Kim (and Kim's nine puppies), and includes many of their stories in this book.

Lucky Dog features sweet and silly stories abou
playful pups and the kids who love them b
some of your favorite authors!

Randi Barrow • Marlane Kennedy
Elizabeth Cody Kimmel • Kirby Larson
C. Alexander London • Leslie Margolis
Jane B. Mason & Sarah Hines Stephens • Ellen Miles
Michael Northrop • Teddy Slater
Tui T. Sutherland • Allan Woodrow